# WHAT PET TO GET?

For Conrad and Imogen, with all my love
Emma xx

A TEMPLAR BOOK

First published in the UK in 2006 by Templar Publishing.
This softback edition published in 2007 by Templar Publishing,
an imprint of The Templar Company plc,
The Granary, North Street, Dorking, Surrey, RH4 1DN, UK
www.templarco.co.uk

Copyright © 2006 by Emma Dodd

First softback edition, second impression

ISBN 978-1-84011-547-5

Edited by Beth Harwood

Printed in Hong Kong

templar publishing

# WHAT PET TO GET?

Emma Dodd

"Let's get a pet," said Jack one day.
"I **promise** I'll look after it."

"If you like, dear," replied his mother
absent-mindedly.
"**What** pet should we get?"

Jack thought about it for a little while.
"I think we should get an elephant," he announced.
"I could **ride** it to school."

"An elephant would be nice, dear," said Mum,
"but not very practical.
How would we take it on holiday?"

"On the roof-rack, of course," said Jack.

"I don't think so, dear," said Mum.
"It might squash the car."

"Hmm, maybe **not** an elephant then,"
said Jack.

"What about a lion?" he said.
"I'd remember to **feed**
it **every** day."

"That would be super, dear,"
replied Mum,
"but lions do have very
**big** appetites...

...and anyway, it would frighten the postman."

"Hmm, I hadn't thought of **that**," said Jack.

Jack thought some more.

"I think we should get a polar bear," he said.
"It would make a **great** playmate."

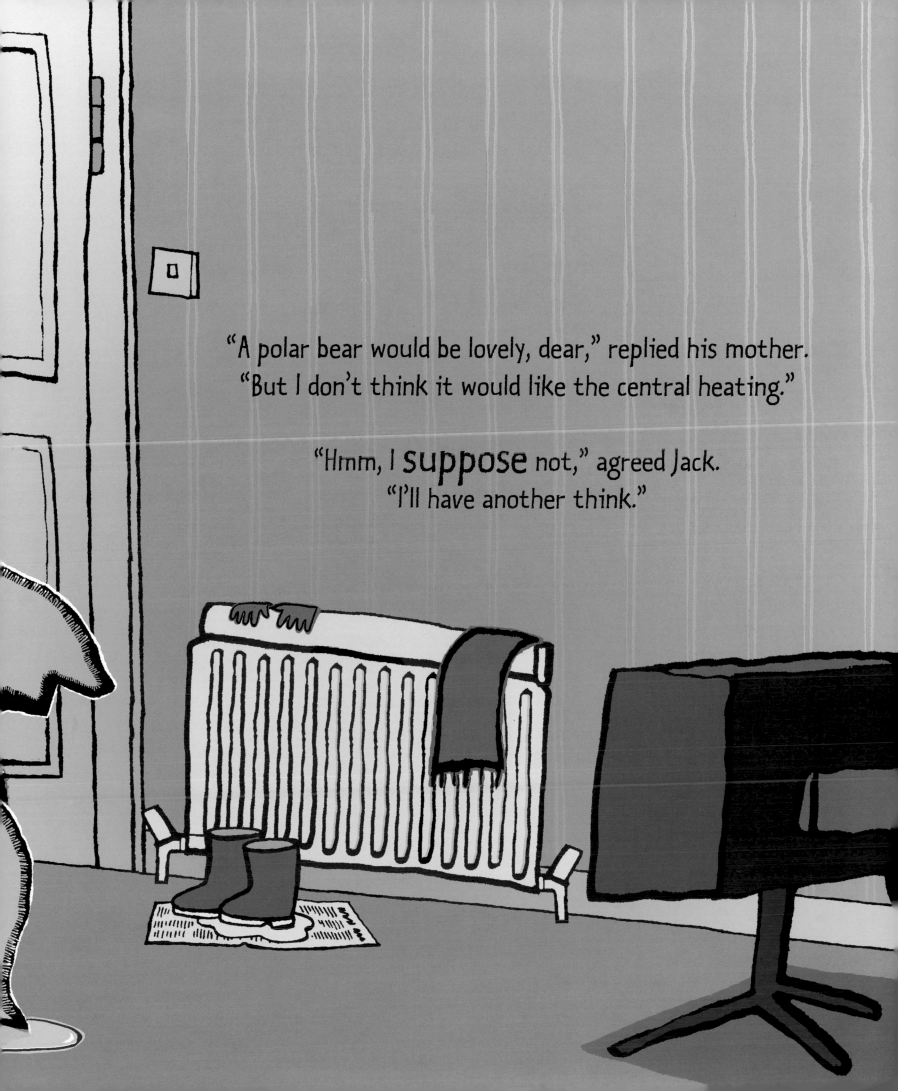

"A polar bear would be lovely, dear," replied his mother.
"But I don't think it would like the central heating."

"Hmm, I **suppose** not," agreed Jack.
"I'll have another think."

Jack thought some more.
What pet to get?

"Could we get a Tyrannosaurus Rex?"
he asked.

"I could take it for **walkies**."

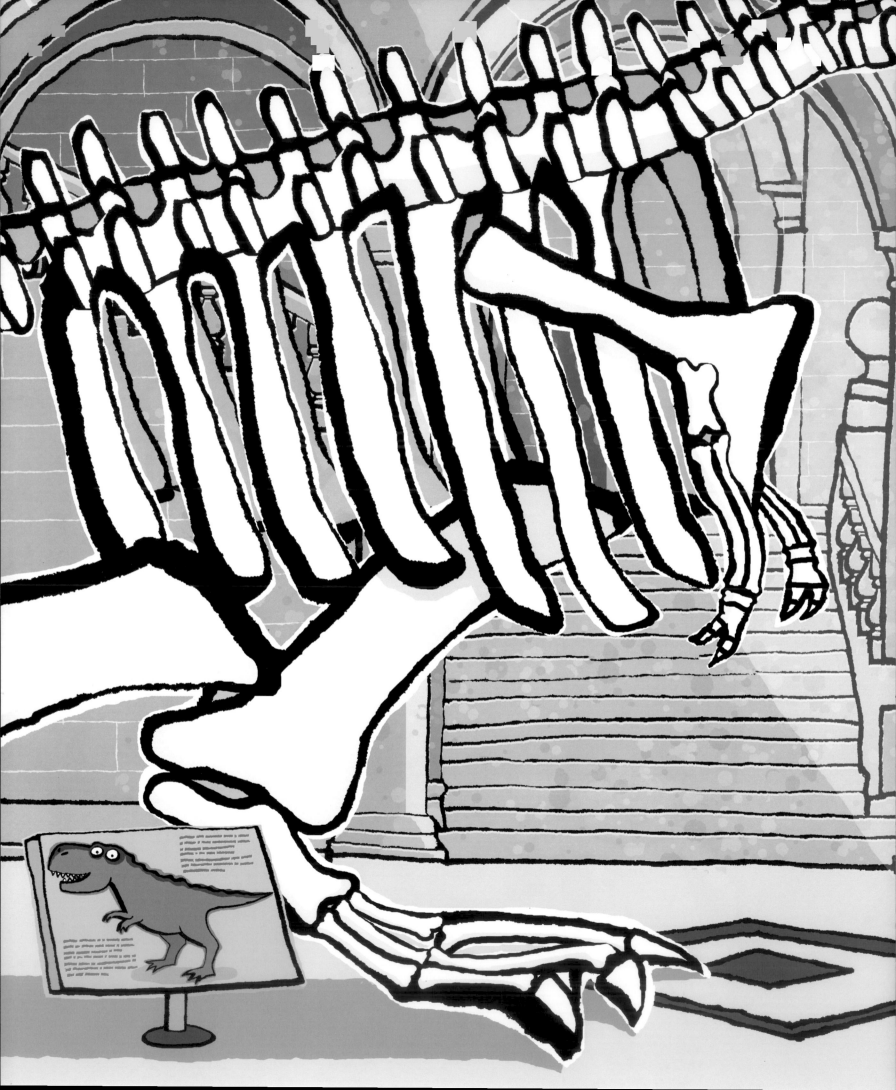

"That **would** have been a great idea, dear," replied Mum, "but unfortunately the Tyrannosaurus Rex has been **extinct** for sixty-five million years."

"What a shame," said Jack. "Well, what about...

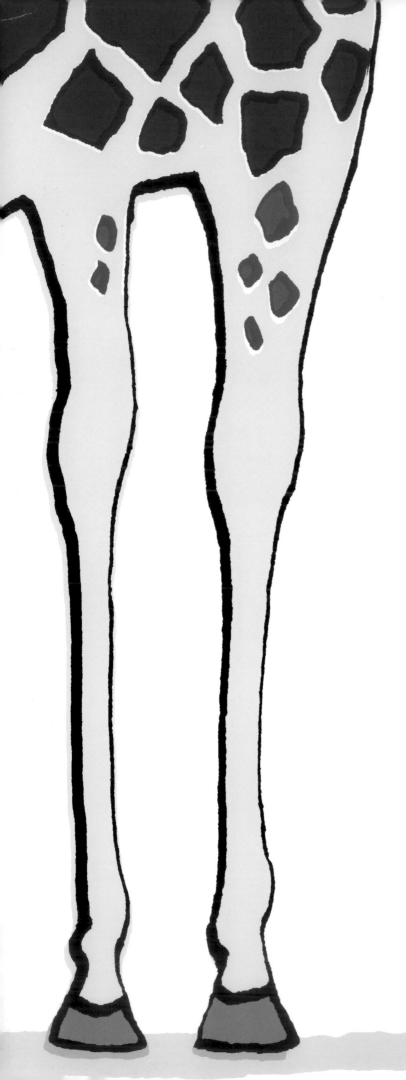

...a giraffe?"

"Too tall!"

"I suppose a **shark** is out of the question?"

"Yes, dear," sighed Mum.
"Perhaps you could try to think of something less...
**exotic**."

Early the next morning, Jack announced,

"I've got it!
Let's get a dog!"

"That's an **excellent** idea, dear,"
said Mum.
"We'll go this morning and choose...